By Sam Watkins Illustr

CREATURE TEACHER

GOES WILD

STONE ARCH BOOKS
a capstone imprint

To Mom. For letting me run wild, but always making sure I did my homework first — S.W.

Creature Teacher Goes Wild is published by Stone Arch Books,
A Capstone Imprint
1710 Roe Crest Drive
North Mankato, Minnesota 56003
www.mycapstone.com

Text copyright © Sam Watkins 2015
Illustrations copyright © David O'Connell 2015
Published in American English in 2018 by Stone Arch Books

Creature Teacher Goes Wild was originally published in English in 2015. This translation
is published by arrangement with Oxford University Press.

Library of Congress Cataloging-in-Publication Data is available
on the Library of Congress website.

ISBN: 978-1-4965-5703-2 (Library Binding)
ISBN: 978-1-4965-5684-4 (Paperback)
ISBN: 978-1-4965-5707-0 (eBook PDF)

Summary:
Jake's class is going to Wilf's Wild Adventure Park, a super fun theme park. But things
get MUCH too wild when Mr. Hyde gets spooked on the ghost train and transforms into
the naughty Creature! Will Jake and his friends be able to work together to track down
Creature and get him to change back into Mr. Hyde before the truth gets out?

Designer:
Mackenzie Lopez

Printed in Canada.
10407F17

TABLE OF CONTENTS

CHAPTER 1:

WACKY WILF'S WILD ADVENTURE PARK

Zap! Zap! "Eurrrrrgh." Zap! Zap! "Eurrrrrgh." Zap-zap . . .

"Move your head, Barnaby!" Jake said. "I want to see out the window."

"No can do. These zombies won't zap themselves," Barnaby replied, his eyes glued to his phone.

Sighing, Jake left Barnaby to his zombie-zapping and looked down the aisle of the bus. His teacher, Mr. Hyde was at the back, wearing a purple pinstriped suit and strumming a ukulele.

"OK, fifth graders," he bellowed. "One, two, three!

If you're happy that you're going to Wacky Wilf's Wild Adventure Park, clap your hands! If you're happy that you're going to Wacky Wilf's Wild Adventure Park, recite the alphabet backward . . ."

Jake shook his head. "Mr. Hyde really is the craziest, funniest, and best teacher in the world," he murmured out loud.

"Solar system," Nora corrected from her seat across the aisle.

"Universe!" added Woodstock, who was sitting next to her.

6

They all grinned at each other. Mr. Hyde *was* a great teacher. He made lessons fun. And he didn't make his students clean the school toilets with toothbrushes, like some teachers they'd had.

"I just hope he doesn't get *too* excited," Nora whispered. "You know how much he likes singing."

Woodstock looked nervous. "He could turn into Creature!"

Alexis' and Karl's heads popped up over the seat behind Nora and Woodstock.

"What was that about Creature?" Alexis asked.

"Nora thinks Mr. Hyde might change into Creature if he gets too excited," Jake explained.

"He does look pretty excited." Karl pointed back at the loudly singing Mr. Hyde. Jake was alarmed to see that his teacher's ears were looking extremely pink!

"You're right," said Jake. "Maybe one of us should sit near him."

"I'll go and keep an eye on him," Alexis said. "Coming, Karl?"

She and Karl made their way to the back of the bus. The singing soon spread to the whole bus. Jake and Woodstock joined in. It was hard not to when Mr. Hyde was around!

Nora hummed along, her nose in an adventure park flyer. Suddenly she gasped.

"Guys, listen to this!" She read aloud: "'The adventure park and all the rides were designed by eccentric billionaire Wilfred Waldo Wellington, Jr.'"

"Wow. A *billion*aire!" Jake said.

Nora carried on. "'Mr. Wellington prefers to be called Wilf—'"

"Class 5B students! It is rude to gossip!"

They looked up. Mrs. Blunt, the principal, was swaying in the aisle on dangerously high heels, glaring at them.

Jake tried to look invisible but it was surprisingly difficult.

Yesterday Mrs. Blunt had given him two Sad Faces: the first for fidgeting in assembly, the second for groaning when she gave him the first. One more Sad Face and he'd have to work on the Rockery tomorrow, hauling horribly heavy rocks.

"Jake Jones —" Mrs. Blunt started to speak, but the singing drowned her out.

"IF YOU'RE HAPPY AND YOU KNOW IT . . ."

The principal stalked further down the aisle and clapped her hands sharply. The singing died away.

"And you reeeally want to show it. . . ." sang Mr. Hyde, with gusto, eyes closed, on his own. He had not seen Mrs. Blunt.

"MIS-TER HYDE!"

The ukulele made one last chord and fell silent.

"Attention, everyone," the principal barked. "It's very generous of Mr. Wilfred Waldo Wellington, Jr., to invite us to the opening day of his new Adventure Park."

Mrs. Blunt walked down the aisle with her hands clasped behind her back. She continued, "Mr. Wellington is a very important person. If he's impressed with you, he may contribute some money toward the principal statues I'm having placed in the school entrance. So I want you all on your best behavior."

She gave Mr. Hyde a look. "That goes for you too, Mr. Hyde. No experimental teaching today. No horseplay, monkey business, or tomfoolery. Understand?"

"No, Mrs. Blunt. Um, I mean yes, Mrs. Blunt," Mr. Hyde said.

"Hmph. We'll see," sighed Mrs. Blunt.

Mrs. Blunt stomped back to the front of the bus through an uneasy silence. But Mr. Hyde was too excited to stay quiet for long.

"Hey, who knows this one? Aga-doo, doo, doo, push pineapple, shake the tree! Aga-doo, doo, doo, push pineapple, grind coffee . . ."

Jake started to join in, but then stopped. Woodstock's face had gone red and he looked like he was about to explode.

"What's up with Woodstock?" Jake whispered to Nora.

"Mrs. Blunt promised funding for a new art studio," Nora whispered back. "The old one is falling to pieces. Woodstock and some other students have been raising money for it."

"But now she says she's putting all the money toward statues of all the school's principals. Says they're for 'posterity,' whatever that means!" Woodstock fumed.

"It's just a way of getting a statue of herself," Nora muttered.

Jake was shocked. "She can't do that!"

"She can. She's the principal," Woodstock said, staring out of the window from beneath his long bangs. "It's totally uncool. But I don't want to talk about it."

Nora tried to cheer him up. She pointed to the adventure park leaflet.

"Woodstock, there are crocodiles in the Wildlife Zone," she said. "I can speak crocodile, you know: Aa- a- r- r- r- rahhhh- ah- ah- ah- ahhhh."

Barnaby looked up and snickered. "How rude. You can't say that."

Nora glared at him. "That was actually crocodile for 'Nice to meet you.'"

"Nice to *eat* you, is more like it!" Jake joked. Woodstock almost smiled.

Nora went red. "It's true! I've researched it. Crocodiles talk in grunts and croaks.

And sometimes they even roar. Like this: HURRRRAAAAAAAAAHHHHH!"

A cheer had erupted at the back of the bus.

"LOOK! A sign for Wilfy Wildo's Wacky Whatsit Park!" Mr. Hyde said too quickly.

Jake turned. His teacher was bouncing up and down and pointing excitedly out of the window.

"We're nearly there! Oh I can't *wait* to go on Ziggy's Zip Line and the Rushing Rocky Rapids and the Wild West Zone looks cool but I'm not going on the Ghost Train and the roller coaster looks mega-scary . . . and . . . and . . ." Mr. Hyde jumped to his feet and burst into song.

"AGA-DOO . . . DOO . . . OOH! There's another sign, we'll be there in two shakes of a jeeper . . . jeeperrrr . . ."

An alarm bell rang in Jake's head.

Mr. Hyde had gone very red . . .

Too red! His ears weren't pink any more —
they were starting to glow!

Alexis and Karl were too busy looking out
of the window to notice.

"What's that burning rubber smell?" asked
Nora, sniffing.

Jake leapt to his feet. *Mr. Hyde was
changing into Creature!*

CHAPTER 2:

YOUR ADVENTURE BEGINS HERE!

"Mr. Hyde!"

Jake raced up the aisle, grabbing a sick bag he spotted on the way. Karl and Alexis were trying to get the glowing Mr. Hyde to sit down.

"Here!" Jake thrust the bag over his teacher's mouth.

"Breathe, sir."

Mr. Hyde inhaled and exhaled deeply then made a face.

"Ugh!" he said. "Why are you making me sniff tuna sandwiches, Jake?"

"That's my lunch!" A boy from Class 5A shoved Jake aside and grabbed the bag.

Jake put his hands up. "Sorry . . ."

Karl and Alexis pulled Mr. Hyde back into his seat just as Nora and Woodstock hustled to the scene.

"Is he OK?" Nora asked.

They all looked at Mr. Hyde. He looked a bit pink, but he wasn't glowing anymore.

"What was that bag thing about, Jake?" Mr. Hyde questioned.

"Sir, you were *glowing!*" Nora whispered.

"Glowing? Thank you, Nora. It's my new skin care regime . . . Oh, I see. You thought I was changing! Don't worry, I've got this Creature thing under control. *Jeepers, we're HERE!*"

The cry went up. "WE'RE HERE!"

Jake raced back down the bus to his seat, elbowed Barnaby out of the way, and pressed his nose to the window.

"Hey!" Barnaby protested. "You made me miss the Head Zombie!"

Jake pointed out of the window. "Forget zombies, Barnaby. We've arrived!"

As the bus rolled to a stop, Mrs. Blunt stood up but was steamrollered back down under a tide of shrieking students.

"SIT DOWN, EVERYONE! Oliver Smith, you get a Sad Face for pushing. And you get one, too, Maisy Maxwell . . ."

Hiiiissssssssss!

The bus doors opened and Jake and his friends spilled into the parking lot. He stopped and gazed around.

In front of him towered a building of gleaming metal and glass. It looked like a humongous spaceport. Across the front was a huge, glowing sign.

WACKY WILF'S WILD
ADVENTURE PARK

"Wooow . . ." he breathed.

"Wooow . . ." breathed fifty-one other awestruck students.

"Wowsers!" Mr. Hyde exclaimed. He turned to Miss Trimble, Class 5A's easily

irritated teacher. "It looks cool, doesn't it, Miss Trimble?"

Miss Trimble hesitated. "It looks, um, clean," she said finally.

Mrs. Blunt marched everyone into the spaceport building and across a spotless silver floor to a desk. A sign above it read:

YOUR ADVENTURE
BEGINS HERE!

A man in a spacesuit came around to stamp everyone's hands. With each stamped hand,the kids got louder with excitement.

"QUIET!" Mrs. Blunt bellowed.

The chatter faded.

"You will be placed in groups. You will stay

with your group
all day. No one is
to go off on their
own, unless they
wish to do time on
the Rockery. Each group
will consist of six students
and one responsible adult.
Read out the groups, Miss
Trimble."

Miss Trimble shuffled
forward.

"Group 1. Nora Newton,
Karl McQueen, Woodstock Stone . . ."

Jake crossed his fingers. *Please let me be
with my friends . . .*

"Alexis Williams, Barnaby McCrumb . . .
and Jake Jones. And your responsible adult:
Mr. Hyde."

Jake high-fived Karl and Woodstock. They looked around for Mr. Hyde, but he was nowhere to be seen.

A surge of cold fear went through Jake. *Surely he hasn't changed, has he?* He looked at the others. "We have to find Mr. Hyde, quick!"

"Don't panic — there he is," Karl said.

Mr. Hyde was bounding toward them, waving a large piece of paper.

"Sir, please don't go off on your own," Nora began.

"From now on I will stick to you like chewing gum on your shoe," Mr. Hyde rhymed. "OK, are we ready for adventures? I've got a map."

They all crowded around.

Mr. Hyde scratched his head. "Hmmm, I can't quite . . . what's this big pink blob?"

"A whale?" Karl suggested.

Nora shook her head. "An ice cream cone."

There was another bark from Mrs. Blunt.

"One final thing. I want everyone back here at one o'clock on the dot for the grand opening ceremony. I will do a head count at that time." She made a grim look. "If anyone is missing, or is even half a millisecond late, there will be trouble with a capital 'R'! Do I make myself clear?"

A sea of blank, confused faces gazed at the principal.

"Oh, I get it!" Nora exclaimed. "'R' is for 'Rockery,'" she called.

"One person remembered her brain this morning," snapped Mrs. Blunt. "OK, everyone, you may go. Oh, before your group leaves, Miss Trimble, I want a word with you and Amelia."

As the groups began to head off, Jake heard a loud, mean voice.

"MAKE WAY, PEOPLE! Mrs. Blunt wants to speak to me!"

Jake looked around. A smug girl with scraped-back blond hair was barging through the crowd — Amelia Trotter-Hogg, most annoying person in the universe. Jake saw Amelia elbow Nora in the back as she walked past their group. Nora yelped.

"Whoops, didn't see you there, Boring Nora," Amelia snickered.

"Say sorry, Amelia," Jake said, gritting his teeth.

"Flaky Jake sticking up for Boring Nora — how *sweet*." Amelia bounced off.

Jake felt rage building up in his stomach. He started to go after her, but Nora grabbed his arm and held him back.

"Don't, Jake. You'll get in trouble."

Jake reluctantly turned back to the others, who were still trying to understand the map.

"Where shall we go first?" Alexis asked.

Mr. Hyde peered at the map. "How about the Alien Zone? There, look. A picture of an alien . . ."

Jake tried to listen, but he was still fuming about Amelia. He looked over to where Amelia, Mrs. Blunt, and Miss Trimble

had their heads together. As he watched, all three of them looked up and seemed to stare directly at him and his group! He flushed and looked away quickly. *Why are they looking over here?* Jake wondered. *Is Amelia trying to get Class 5B students in trouble?*

"Come on, Jake!" called Mr. Hyde.

His group was moving on. He cast another glance at Amelia. She held his gaze for a few seconds, smirking nastily.

"JAKE!" his group called after him.

He ran to catch up with the others. *It isn't only Mr. Hyde I'll need to keep an eye on today*, he thought.

CHAPTER 3:

THE FLOWER POWER FAIRY ZONE

"Are we almost there?" Woodstock asked. "My feet hurt."

Jake and his group had been walking for a quarter of an hour and still had not found the Alien Zone. That would have been bad enough, but ever since leaving the entrance, Amelia's group had been trailing along just behind them. Jake could hear her irritating snicker almost constantly.

"They must be going to the Alien Zone, too," Nora whispered to Jake.

"Yeah, maybe." Jake thought about the secretive conversation between Amelia, Mrs. Blunt, and Miss Trimble at the entrance. *Was it coincidence that Amelia's group was going exactly the same way as them?* Jake thought. *Or was there something else to it?*

"Ooof! Sorry . . ." Jake grunted.

Jake had bumped into Mr. Hyde, who had screeched to a halt just in front of him.

"That's odd," Mr. Hyde said, squinting at a sign over the path.

> ## THE FLOWER
> ## POWER FAIRY ZONE

Jake and his friends looked at each other.

"There's no way I'm going in there," Barnaby snorted. "You promised me aliens."

Barnaby had a point. The Flower Power Fairies were characters in a little kid's show. At the end of each episode they shouted, '*Peace and love!*' Jake's sister, Connie, loved it, but she was only three years old. Jake hated it.

Mr. Hyde looked at the map, puzzled.

"But there are pictures of aliens . . ."

Nora took the map. "Those aren't aliens, they're flowers!"

"PEACE AND LOVE!" Amelia shouted.

Jake winced. Amelia's group had arrived. She looked at the Flower Power Fairy Zone sign, then smirked at Barnaby.

"Big rides too scary for you, McCrumb?"

Barnaby glared at her. "Following us around again, Hogg-Trotter?"

"IT'S TROTTER-HOGG!" Amelia snarled.

"Calm down, everyone," Mr. Hyde soothed as Miss Trimble bustled up. "We were looking for the Alien Zone, but somehow we've gotten lost."

"Oh yes, Mr. Hyde, the map is very confusing, isn't it?" Miss Trimble said. "But this zone looks nice."

Nora was still looking at the map. "I *think* we can go through here to the Alien Zone."

"Fantabulous! Off we go, then!" Mr. Hyde exclaimed. Ignoring Barnaby's grumbling, he marched under the sign, followed by Jake and his friends.

Jake blinked as a bright rainbow of colors struck his eyes.

Everywhere, monstrous, brightly painted flowers sprouted as tall as trees. Fountains of colored water sprang up as they walked past, with shimmering rainbows hovering around them. Miniature carousels revolved slowly to high-pitched music.

Smiley people dressed in flower costumes wandered about.

"Peace and love!" sang a daisy to Barnaby.

Barnaby scowled. "Whatever."

As they made their way across the Flower Power Fairy Zone, Jake could still hear Amelia's voice just behind them. His stomach tightened. *I won't let Amelia ruin our day!*

He made a decision. "Let's lose Amelia," he muttered to the others. "She's definitely up to something."

They nodded in agreement.

Jake started to walk faster. So did Woodstock, Nora, Alexis, and Karl.

"That's the spirit!" Mr. Hyde said.

But it was no use. The faster they walked, the faster Amelia's group followed.

Jake grew more and more annoyed. And Barnaby wasn't helping matters, either. Barnaby was slowing them down because his eyes were still glued to his zombie game.

As they dashed past a carousel, Jake looked over his shoulder. Amelia's group had fallen behind, and Amelia seemed to be arguing with Miss Trimble.

Suddenly, off to one side, Jake saw a little flower-covered archway.

"Quick! In there!" he said to the others. With any luck, Amelia wouldn't see where they went.

One by one, they ducked under the arch. Inside, a lady dressed as a daffodil fairy was sitting on a toadstool, pouring glitter into different pots. She looked up.

"Peace and love!" the daffodil fairy sang.

"Peace and love to you, too," Mr. Hyde said politely.

Zap zap! Barnaby wandered through the arch, still busy destroying zombies.

Zap, zap, aargh . . . TAN-TARA! TAN-TARA! TAN-TARA!

Barnaby nearly dropped his phone in fright as trumpets started to toot and bells started to sound all around them!

The daffodil jumped off her toadstool.

"You're the Lucky Thirteenth visitor to the Flower Power Bower!" she cried, prancing merrily toward Barnaby with a pair of silver wings and a pot of fairy dust. "You've won a pair of wings, dear!"

"Aaaargh, get off!" Barnaby squawked, pushing the wings away. But the daffodil was not put off that easily.

"A touch of fairy dust, then?" she cried.

She sprinkled a handful of fairy dust over Barnaby's head.

Barnaby's face turned an angry shade of glittery red. The fairy looked less happy.

"You're not . . . allergic to glitter, are you?" she asked nervously.

There was a cackle of horrid laughter from behind them.

Jake closed his eyes. *Great. Just what we need.* Amelia was standing in the archway, her group at her side.

"Oooh look, it's Sparkly McCrumb, the Cookie Fairy!" Amelia giggled.

Barnaby looked as if he might explode. "THAT'S IT!" he shouted. "I've had enough of this!" He pushed his way past Amelia and her group and stormed out of the Flower Power Bower.

"Barnaby!" Jake called.

But Mr. Hyde stopped him. "Give him a second to cool off outside."

Amelia looked at the daffodil fairy. "Hey, if he doesn't want the wings, can I have them?"

The daffodil looked uncertain.

"Well, I'm not supposed to —"

"Oh come on!" Amelia grabbed the wings.

The daffodil tried to hold on to them, but Amelia wrestled them out of her grasp.

The daffodil gave up. She knew when she'd been beaten. "Well, all right," she sighed. "Just don't tell anyone! Now, I need a photo for the Hall of Fairy Fame. Wait there while I get the camera." The daffodil skipped off, saying, "Peace and love!" as she went.

"Let's go and get Barnaby," Mr. Hyde said to Jake and his classmates. Amelia stayed put. She grabbed a mirror from her bag and started smoothing down hairs that didn't need smoothing.

They all ducked through the archway.

"This," said Woodstock, "is officially becoming a nightmare."

Karl laughed. "Barnaby would probably agree."

Jake looked around. "Hang on," he said. "Where is he?"

Barnaby had vanished!

CHAPTER 4:

WICKED WILF'S
GHOULISH GHOST TRAIN

"BARNABYYYYYYY!" shouted Jake.

They walked all around the Flower Power Fairy Zone calling for Barnaby, but he didn't appear. Finally, Mr. Hyde stopped them.

"We'll have to go back and report him missing," he said.

Jake groaned. *All that way, for nothing!* He trudged gloomily after the others, as they headed back to the entrance.

But everything looked different.
The tall, colorful flowers had turned into
taller, menacing trees with grinning skulls
painted on them. Jake ran to catch up
with the others.

"We didn't come this way," he said to Nora. "Where are we?"

Nora looked at the map. "It's not clear, but I think we're in Spookyville."

Suddenly, Karl gave a shout.

"There's Barnaby!"

Way ahead, on the path, Jake saw the unmistakable figure of his classmate. Barnaby stared at them for a moment. Then he started running.

"BARNABYYYYYY!" yelled Mr. Hyde and tore off after him. As Jake tried to keep up, he saw first Barnaby, and then Mr. Hyde, swerve off the path. By the time Jake and the others reached the end of the path, both of them had disappeared.

"Where'd they go?" panted Nora.

"In there, maybe?" Karl pointed to a black building. Splattered across the front in dripping red letters were the words:

WICKED WILF'S
GHOULISH GHOST TRAIN

They raced into the building and through a turnstile into a dark corridor. Ahead, Jake could see Mr. Hyde at the back of a line of people, craning to peer over the sea of heads. They ran to join him.

"Is he there, sir?" Jake asked.

"I think he jumped the line," Mr. Hyde said. "But it's too dark to see . . . what is this place?"

"The ghost train, sir."

Mr. Hyde's face drained of color. For a minute, Jake thought he was going to turn back. But a sober look came into his eye.

"You're a responsible adult, Hydey," Mr. Hyde muttered to himself. "There's a lost student in there — probably terrified out of his mind — and it's your duty to find him!"

They reached the front of the line as an empty train rattled up. Jake saw that it consisted of three small carriages. Karl and Woodstock got in the first carriage, Nora and Alexis in the second one. Jake and a very pale-looking Mr. Hyde slid into the last carriage. The train started moving.

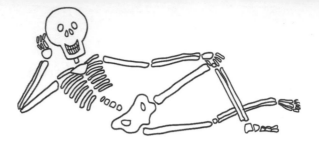

"We're not going to spend all day chasing Barnaby, are we?" Alexis grumbled, as they chugged toward a curtain.

"Barnaby's upset," Mr. Hyde said. "He's your friend, and I'm a firm believer in friends sticking together."

Alexis made a face. "But he didn't stick with us!"

"Friends stick together," Mr. Hyde repeated, as the train plunged into a dark tunnel.

"Together . . . together . . . together," came an eerie echo.

Everyone jumped. Mr. Hyde yelped and pulled his jacket over his head.

Then, with a rattle, a plastic skeleton swung out of the wall toward them.

Karl and Woodstock burst out laughing. "Scary, not!" said Karl.

Nora snorted. "That skeleton is wrong. There are actually 206 bones in a human skeleton."

"Leave it to you to spot that!" Jake grinned.

After a few more fake skeletons had popped out of the walls, the train emerged into what looked like a dimly lit dining hall. A grandfather clock ticked loudly in a corner.

With a groan, the train came to a halt.

"Why have we stopped?" Mr. Hyde yelped, peeking out from under his coat.

"I don't know," Jake said, puzzled.

DONG*!!!*

The deafening sound shattered the silence. The grandfather clock was chiming!

Jake clapped his hands over his ears as the racket continued.

DONG*!* DONG*!* DONG*!!!*

It chimed twelve times. As the twelfth dong died dismally away, ghoulish figures emerged from the shadows.

"Nnnnneeeuuuuuurrrrrghhh . . ." moaned the figures.

"Zombies!" Woodstock shouted.

The zombies lurched toward the train with jerky, mechanical movements. Jake realized they must be dummies. *They look pretty realistic, though,* he thought. They stopped

an arm's length from the train and stood
flailing and moaning.

"Euuuurrrrghhhh!" moaned the
zombie nearest to Jake, waving a gruesome,
bloody arm.

Jake laughed. "Euuuurrrrghhhh to you,
too! I wonder what it's made of . . ."

He grabbed the zombie's arm and
squeezed it hard.

RRRRRRRRRIPPPPPP!

The zombie arm came off in Jake's hand!

"Aaargh, my arm!" the zombie groaned, staggering back.

Jake felt an icy shock zap through his veins.

"IT'S REAL!" Nora shrieked. Everyone gasped.

The zombie lurched toward Jake again.

"You have angered the Head Zombie!" the zombie howled. "Now he will eat your braaaaaaaaaaaiiiins . . ."

Mr. Hyde shot back under his coat. Heart racing, Jake brandished the arm he was still clutching. It was some kind of hard plastic — good for a weapon.

Plastic . . . his brain whirred. Then it clicked. *Plastic? Of course it's plastic, you nitwit! Zombies aren't real . . .*

"Whack it!" Karl shouted. "Hurry, Jake! Destroy the zombie."

A lightbulb went on in Jake's brain. He knew someone else who liked to destroy zombies. He lowered the arm.

"Take that mask off, Barnaby," said Jake. "I know it's you."

Nora gasped. "*Barnaby?*"

The zombie laughed and took off his mask.

"Ha, ha. Had you fooled for a minute, didn't I?" Barnaby was smirking.

"You'll get us all in trouble, Barnaby," said Nora angrily.

Barnaby shrugged. "Yeah, yeah. It was funny, though . . ."

Jake whirled around to speak to Mr. Hyde.

"We've found him . . . Sir?"

Mr. Hyde had retreated completely inside his coat. Almost like he'd shrunk.

"Mr. Hyde!" said Jake, tugging at his teacher's sleeve. "OWWWW!"

Jake jerked his hand back. The coat was red hot! A strange glow came from beneath it. Sucking his burnt fingers, Jake realized what was happening.

"Quick, tap your leg, sir!" he cried. Mr. Hyde could sometimes stop himself from changing by tapping his leg.

But it was too late.

All six students stared open-mouthed as orange rays of light began to stream from the buttonholes and sleeves of the coat. Smoke poured from the neck, and Jake could smell burning rubber.

FAAAAAAAAAAAAAARRRRRT!

Wheeeeeeee · · · · · · · · · ·

POP! POP! POP!

BANG!

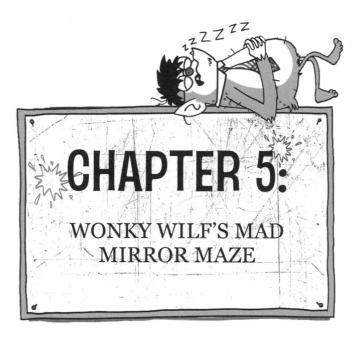

CHAPTER 5:

WONKY WILF'S MAD MIRROR MAZE

Nora leapt to her feet. "Noooooooooo . . ."

Barnaby dove for cover behind one of the carriages.

"JAKE! GET OUT!" shouted Alexis.

Jake leapt over into Alexis and Nora's carriage and ducked down . . .

Mr. Hyde's coat burst like an over-inflated balloon as the fart filled it. A rain of purple fabric fluttered down on Jake and his classmates' heads.

Silence.

Even the mechanical zombies had stopped groaning. Jake, Nora, and Alexis slowly lifted their heads and stared at each other. No one moved.

"What's happening?" Jake heard Karl whisper from the front car.

"Has he . . . changed?" Woodstock whispered.

Very carefully, Jake pulled himself up and peered into the last carriage. As the cloud of smoke cleared, he saw a small, hairy creature squatting on the seat where Mr. Hyde's coat had been moments before. It squinted at Jake through black-rimmed glasses.

Mr. Hyde's glasses.

Jake swallowed. The worst had happened. Mr. Hyde had changed into Creature! Jake reached behind him.

"Someone give me a bag, quick!"

If he could just . . . he felt a bag pushed into his hand. He slowly held it out over Creature, who was nibbling experimentally on the plastic zombie arm.

"Niiiiice Creature," whispered Jake, leaning over.

"YIK!" Creature threw the arm away. It whacked Jake on the head.

"OW!" Jake lost his balance and toppled into the back carriage. He tried to grab the startled Creature as he fell, but missed.

"Jeeppppppeeeeeerrrrrrrrrrr!"

Creature bounded off the train. Straight into Barnaby, who was crawling out from under the table.

Barnaby squawked. "Get off!"

Creature grabbed Barnaby's ears and swung himself up onto his head.

"YOOOWWWW!" howled Barnaby.

Every one of Creature's hairs stood on end. He shot off Barnaby's head like a rocket-propelled hedgehog and landed on a huge chandelier that was hanging right above the train. The chandelier lurched dangerously. Creature chattered crossly at Barnaby.

"My ears have stretched!" Barnaby groaned, rubbing them.

"It's your own fault!" Nora exclaimed. "You made him change."

Barnaby shrugged. "Blah, blah."

Creeeeeeeeeeeeeeakkkkkk . . .

". . . blah . . ." Barnaby's voice trailed away. He stared up at the old, swaying chandelier.

"What's that?" Nora rubbed her eyes. Jake coughed. Bits of plaster were falling on his head. He looked back up and sucked his breath in sharply.

Creature's weight was too much for the chandelier. Slowly but surely, it was ripping out of the ceiling.

"It's coming down!" Alexis screamed.

Jake jumped up. "Off the train!" he yelled, but he was thrown back in his seat as the train suddenly jerked forward!

Creeeeeeeeeeakkkk . . .

With a squawk, Creature somersaulted off the chandelier.

CRAAAAASH!!

A mangled mess of metal landed in a shower of plaster on the track behind the moving train, missing Jake by inches. As the train lurched into a tunnel, Jake caught a glimpse of Creature disappearing through a side door, followed by Barnaby.

Then they were plunged into darkness.

For what seemed like ages, the train bolted along in the dark. At last, it emerged into the light and shook to a halt at the station.

Jake scrambled out, then stopped. "This isn't where we got on!"

The platform was lined with mirrors. A voice boomed through a speaker.

"Welcome to Wonky Wilf's Mad Mirror Maze! Can you find your way to the front entrance without losing your mind?"

Jake turned to the others. "We've got to catch Creature," he said.

"And Barnaby," Nora reminded him. "I saw them both go through a side door."

Jake nodded. "We need to find them before the opening ceremony!"

"But how?" Woodstock asked.

"That announcement just said there was another entrance. We'll go through the maze and get out that way and start to look," Karl said.

They ran along the platform to a door. Jake pushed it open and stepped through.

"Whoa," Jake gasped.

He was in a room full of hundreds, maybe thousands, of Jakes!

An army of Noras appeared behind the army of Jakes. Then hundreds of Karls and Woodstocks, and finally Jake saw Alexis reflected over and over. They were all oohing and ahhing. Every time Jake moved, his reflections moved too. It made him dizzy.

"OK," said Jake, looking around. "That way."

He walked forward. WHACK! Straight into a mirror.

"This way!" called Nora. Jake tried to follow what he thought was Nora, but a mirror blocked his way. He'd been following her reflection!

"Jake! Where are you?" he heard Alexis call. He saw a flash of her red soccer shirt out of the corner of his eye, then nothing. Karl and Woodstock, too, had vanished.

Don't panic, Jake sternly told his reflections. Suddenly there was a movement behind him! A dark shape flashed briefly into view in one of the mirrors, then vanished.

He whirled around. *Was that Creature?*

"Flawless, absolutely flawless."

Someone was murmuring from around the corner! He peered round.

Amelia!

Jake quickly whipped his head back. Miss Trimble was probably not far away then. And if Creature *was* in here . . . Jake peered around the corner again.

Amelia was making kissy faces in a mirror. She bent down to fish around in her bag and brought out a pair of pink sunglasses.

Jake started to back away. But then he stopped. The mirror Amelia had been looking in was being slid to one side!

A furry face with glasses appeared.

Jake staggered backward. *Creature!*

Amelia stood up, sunglasses on. She looked in the mirror.

"Mwah!" She smacked her lips.

BUURRRRRRRRRRRP! Creature replied.

"ARGHHHHHHHHHHHHH!"

Amelia screamed so loudly, Jake thought every mirror in the maze would shatter!

Creature cackled. Then he grabbed Amelia's sunglasses and disappeared.

Amelia stared at the hole where Creature had vanished and let out a howl."BARNABY MCCRUMB! I know that was you!"

She walked off down a dark, twisty-turny corridor lined with all kinds of strange mirrors at odd angles. Jake followed at what he thought was a safe distance. But suddenly there was a Creaturish cackle behind him. Amelia heard it too and whirled around.

Jake had no time to hide.

"Jake Jones!" Amelia cried. "*You* took my sunglasses?"

Jake was about to deny this, when he saw Amelia's face go deathly white. She didn't say a word to Jake, just stared. She pointed a trembling finger.

"Behind you . . ."

Jake turned around, very slowly. His mouth dropped open.

In the darkness behind him stood a gigantic, menacing, hairy shape!

CHAPTER 6:

GLADYS'S GLABBERANTHIAN GLOOP

The monster opened its mouth in a yawn showing two rows of sharp, sharp teeth.

THUD

Amelia fainted.

Jake started to back away then turned to flee. Two more enormous figures with stretched-out limbs and huge heads were coming from the other side. He was trapped!

But . . . wait! One of these monsters had long, floppy bangs. The other was wearing a white lab coat and glasses.

Woodstock and Nora! The mirrors had distorted them. So the other figure must be . . .

"CREATURE!" Jake sprinted toward the monster.

SMACK!

Straight into a mirror.

As he clutched his throbbing nose, it struck him what was happening. He hadn't seen Creature. He had seen Creature's *reflection* in a distorting mirror! Jake looked in the mirror next to him. He looked normal size. Then he took a few steps back. His reflection suddenly slid upward till it was several feet tall. The further away you stood, the taller you got!

Nora and Woodstock hurried up beside him.

"Where's Creature?" Nora asked.

"It was only his reflection," Jake said, exasperated.

At that moment, Alexis and Karl appeared. Karl had a large bruise on his forehead.

"That just happened to us, too!" Alexis explained. "Karl ran headfirst into a mirror!"

She suddenly spotted Amelia, still out cold on the floor.

"Amelia! What happened?" asked Nora.

"She fainted. We'll have to get her out of here," Jake said.

They prodded Amelia until she opened her eyes.

"W-where's the monster?" she murmured, looking around with blurry eyes.

"It wasn't a monster," Jake said. "It was, um, just your reflection. Come on."

Jake and Woodstock pulled Amelia along mirrored halls till they finally found the front entrance. As they went out, Jake saw a figure slouching against the wall looking bored.

It was Barnaby, wearing pink sunglasses!

Amelia went as pink as the sunglasses. She marched up to him and grabbed them.

"I knew it was you who stole them!"

"I didn't steal them! I found them," Barnaby protested, "on the floor in the maze."

"Liar —"

"AMELIA!"

Amelia was interrupted by a shout. Miss Trimble was flapping toward them, the rest of her group trailing after her.

"You shouldn't have run off," she panted. "You know what Mrs. Blunt said!"

Amelia suddenly threw Jake a sly look.

"Yes, teachers must stay with their groups! So where's *your* teacher, Jake Jones?"

"He went . . . to the restroom," Jake said.

"I don't believe you. He's doing something off curriculum again! Mrs. Blunt said —"

"Mrs. Blunt *told* you to keep an eye on Mr. Hyde, didn't she?" Jake exclaimed. "That's why you've been following us."

Miss Trimble wrung her hands. "Children, let's not argue. "

Amelia ignored her. "I'm calling Mrs. Blunt. She gave me her cell phone number in case something like this happened." She reached for her bag.

Her face dropped.

"My bag! I must have left it somewhere in that mirror place!"

"Oh dear!" Miss Trimble exclaimed. She shifted uncomfortably from one foot to the other. "Mr. Hyde's group, wait here. My group, follow me. We will find Amelia's bag together."

As Amelia's group trooped back into the maze, Jake turned to the others.

"I knew it. Mrs. Blunt told Amelia to spy on Mr. Hyde!" he said.

Nora looked worried. "And now she's gone back into the maze, and Creature's in there."

Barnaby jumped up. "No, he's not!" He pointed.

In the distance, Jake saw a brown ball of fur bouncing across the grass toward a huge orange dome that looked like a half-sunken Saturn, a giant ring swooping around it at an angle.

House-sized letters on the ring read:

ALIEN ZONE

"After him!" Jake shouted.

They raced off after Creature. As they neared the dome it got busier and busier. Everyone seemed to be going to the Alien Zone! By the time they had pushed through the crowds Creature had disappeared.

As they reached the entrance, Jake heard a distant shout.

"HEY!"

They turned, to see Amelia and her group galloping after them. Amelia looked as determined as ever.

"Why can't that pony-tailed pest leave us alone?" Karl grumbled.

"She wants an excuse to call Mrs. Blunt," Alexis said. "Let's go."

They ran into the dome. It wasn't called the Alien Zone for nothing!

Aliens of all shapes, sizes ,and colors milled about. Green goggle-eyed ones. Purple pimple-nosed ones. Furry, cute ones. Slimy, not-so cute ones. Small, annoying ones.

Jake realized that a lot of little kids were dressed in alien costumes. There was a quick tug on his sleeve.

"Amelia's catching up!" Nora cried.

Jake glanced back, and caught a glimpse of a blond, pony-tailed head bobbing through the crowd.

"We'll have to hide!" he said.

"But where?" Karl asked.

They all looked around frantically. A few feet away, Jake spotted a little food stand. A handwritten sign on the counter said, "BACK IN 5 MINUTES Gladys."

Jake pointed. "There."

They dashed behind the stand. Barnaby climbed up and dipped his finger in the huge vat of slimy green stuff on the counter.

"Mmm! It's like lime jelly, only goopier."

"Barnaby, GET DOWN!"

Karl and Alexis yanked Barnaby down just as Amelia burst out of the crowd and screeched to a halt a few feet away.

Everyone held their breath.

Jake heard Miss Trimble's voice.

"Are you *sure* they came this way, Amelia?"

"I saw them! Oh Miss, can I call Mrs. Blunt now?"

Suddenly a shadow fell over Jake. With a sinking feeling, he looked up. A large lady in a green alien costume was standing over him, her antennae twitching angrily.

Gladys! Jake realized in dismay.

"Honestly, I leave my stand for five minutes, only to find it's been infested with CHILDREN!" Gladys growled. "Out! All of you. This is not a place for hide-and-seek!"

Red-faced, Jake slowly started to get to his feet. Nora did too.

"Come along, I've got customers to serve!" Gladys leaned over to speak to someone on the other side of the stand. "Won't be a minute, little fellow . . . hey, what are you doing? STOP!"

SPLOOOOOOOSH!!!!

Jake threw himself back down as green gloop sprayed everywhere. Gladys's "customer" had jumped into the vat of Glabberanthian Gloop!

CHAPTER 7:

ZIGGY'S ZIP LINE

The huge vat of gloop teetered one way . . . then the other · · ·

It came to rest with a rattle.

Gladys's mouth fell open. Jake stared up at the vat. Slowly, a glistening green head emerged over the rim.

"Hic!"

Jake's eyes nearly popped out.

CREATURE!

Gladys found her voice. "My beautiful gloop!" She grabbed a large wooden spoon from the counter and advanced on Creature.

Jake leapt up, followed by the others.

"NO!" Nora shouted.

"Don't touch him!" Alexis cried.

"THERE THEY ARE!"

Jake groaned. In his search for Creature, he'd forgotten Amelia! She marched toward the stand, phone in hand, followed by a huffing Miss Trimble.

"No more children over here." Gladys waved the spoon menacingly. "I'm closed."

Amelia waved her phone tauntingly. "Well, you can't stop me." She continued forward.

Miss Trimble fluttered like a confused chicken.

"We're trapped!" gasped Nora.

A rattle made Jake look around. Creature was hauling himself out of the gloop. The vat was starting to lean over . . . further and further . . .

KEERRR-RAAAASH!

. . . he tumbled to the ground in front of the gloop stand.

SPLOOOSH!!!!

Amelia gave a scream that turned into a gurgle as a wave of green gloop knocked her off her feet. With a wet-sounding squelch, Creature bolted off into the crowd.

"Noooo!" wailed Gladys, sinking down to her knees.

Jake shouted to the others.

"Run!"

As one unit, they bolted out from behind the stall, past the chattering Gladys, and sprinted after Creature.

Although he had disappeared into the crowd, it was easy to see where he'd gone from the sticky trail of green gloop.

The trail led into another domed building. Jake read the sign.

ZIGGY'S
ZIP LINE

Karl groaned. "Creature on a zip line? Sounds like trouble!"

Barnaby smirked. "Sounds like fun!"

At that moment a loud voice broke across the noise of the crowd.

"Slow down, Amelia! Monsters? Green gloop? You're losing your mind . . ."

"It's Mrs. Blunt! In here!" Jake cried.

They all scurried into Ziggy's Zip Line dome. Jake peeked back out.

He saw Mrs. Blunt bulldozing through the crowd, phone pressed to her ear. She stopped in front of the zip line building, just as a sticky, green, wild-eyed Amelia appeared.

"They're bound to come in here," he heard Woodstock whisper. "We'll have to go up to the zip line!"

They ran to the elevator, but there was a very long line.

"We can't wait," said Nora in a panicky voice. "Oh, look!"

She pointed to a trail of green footprints on the floor. They followed it to a small door. "Do You Dare Take The Stair?" a sign above it asked.

Jake opened the door.

"We dare!" he said and began to climb.

Ten minutes later, Jake didn't feel so daring. It was the longest, wobbliest staircase ever, and it creaked horribly at every step. Finally they reached a metal platform. It swayed as they stepped onto it, making Jake's stomach lurch.

"Eurrgh," said Nora, closing her eyes. "How high are we?"

"I've been higher," muttered Barnaby, staring hard at his shoes.

"Where's Creature?" Alexis asked.

Jake looked around. From the far side of the platform two thick wires snaked across the dome. In front of them stood a line of children, some wearing alien costumes. As Jake watched, two kids in costumes were being strapped into chairs hanging from the wires. One of them was wriggling around a

lot, to the annoyance of
the alien-suited man
trying to strap him in.

*Wait, there's
something weird
about that kid.* Jake
looked closer.

He was wearing
thick glasses. And he looked
green, furry, and . . . *slimy?*

"Creature! He's going on the zip line!"
cried Jake.

Nora gasped. "We've got to stop him!"

Ignoring angry mutters from the crowd, they
started to push their way to the front of the
line. Jake saw the zip line man grab a lever.

"STOP!" he yelled.

Too late.

"JEEPPPPPPPPPP PPPPPERRRRRRRRRR!"

Creature screamed as he shot off down the wire at top speed, slimy green fur flying out behind him.

Jake ran up to the zip line man. "Excuse me."

The man put his hand up. "No line jumping!" he said sternly. "Who's next?"

Alexis broke in. "Please, one of those kids who just went down is, um, my little brother. We've got to go after him! He just ran off."

The man looked alarmed. "Oh no! Well, I suppose you'd better go next, then. You'll have to go two at a time."

There was grumbling from the crowd.

"Barnaby, we'll go first," said Jake.

Barnaby didn't look happy about this, but Alexis pushed him forward. "You've been higher," she reminded him, grinning.

The man strapped them in.

"Ready?" he asked. Jake gulped and nodded. Barnaby shut his eyes tightly.

"Here goes . . ."

The lever was pulled. Jake felt his chair jerk forward, then with a surge of excitement, he slid out into space, slowly at first but gaining speed, until he could hardly catch his breath.

Crowds of ant-sized people scurried below him. He sailed above the highest loop of the roller coaster, just as a car full of screaming people sped over the top!

"Woooooo-hooooooooo!" he yelled to Barnaby on the other wire.

Barnaby didn't woo-hoo back.

In fact, Barnaby had his eyes closed and looked as green as an alien.

WHOOMPH! They flew right out through the hole in the dome! The shock of the cold outdoor air stung Jake's eyes. He was still gaining speed. Eyes streaming, he gasped to see that he was rocketing straight toward a big wooden building . . . he could just make out the words BUCKAROO BAR. He was going to crash straight into it!

Jake screwed his eyes shut and waited for the bang, but then he felt his chair slowing down. Slower . . . slower . . . and he came to a gentle stop.

A cowgirl was waiting to help them down.

"Howdy, folks!" she said. "Welcome to the Wild, Wild West Zone!"

Barnaby groaned. "Fetch a bucket. I'm going to be sick!"

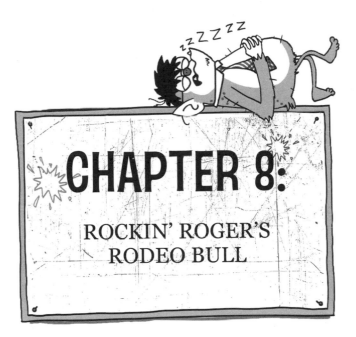

CHAPTER 8:

ROCKIN' ROGER'S RODEO BULL

BLEEEUUURGH! Yuck. Poor Barnaby's breakfast had come out to say hello.

"Good thing I've got loads of buckets," the cowgirl said to Jake as Barnaby groaned into his bucket. "One of the kids who just came down tried to run off with three!"

"Which kid?" Jake asked, suddenly alert.

"Green furry costume, glasses. He's somewhere over there . . ."

She jerked her head toward the Buckaroo Bar. Sitting against the wall, with his head in a bucket, was Creature!

Every muscle in Jake's body tensed. He glanced at the cowgirl, but she had gone back to helping Barnaby. Looking up he saw Alexis and Karl whizzing down the zip line, but he couldn't wait for them.

Jake took his coat off and tiptoed toward Creature.

Slowly, easy does it . . . Jake held his breath. *Closer . . . closer . . .*

"JAKE!"

A shout made him jump. *Alexis!* She and Karl were getting off the zip line.

"Shh . . ." Jake began, but it was too late.

Creature shot bolt upright, the bucket still on his head. With a tinny squeak, he bounded off toward the —

CRASH!!

He bounced off the wall of the Buckaroo Bar, staggered to his feet and ran the other way.

DOOF!!!

Straight into Karl. Surprised, Karl tried to grab him, but Creature slipped through his fingers like a bar of slimy green soap.

"Surround him!" Jake shouted, just as Woodstock and Nora ran up.

Creature wrenched the bucket off his head and stood panting, his slimy fur sticking out in all directions. Karl and Woodstock edged forward. Alexis and Nora edged forward. Jake edged forward.

"NOW!"

They pounced.

PAAAAAAAAAAAARP!

A cloud of lime green gas exploded from Creature's rear end, just as Jake hurled the coat over him. All five of them pinned the squawking Creature to the ground.

After a minute, he stopped wriggling and started to make a rumbling noise.

Nora looked worried. "Is he OK?"

"Maybe he's changing back!" Woodstock said hopefully.

Jake peered under the coat. Creature was snoring.

"He's asleep," Jake said, astonished.

"Ahhh, sweet!" Nora patted Jake's slimy, gloop-covered coat. Just then, Barnaby appeared.

"Where've you been?" Alexis asked, glaring at him. "Running off again, I bet."

Barnaby said nothing.

Jake saw that he still looked a bit green. "He's here now, anyway," he said quickly. "More importantly, we have to think about how to get Creature to change back into Mr. Hyde before one o'clock."

"Sing to him? That worked before," Karl suggested.

"Good idea. But we'll have to wake him up," Jake said.

"Hey!" The cowgirl called over. "There's a competition at Rockin' Roger's Rodeo to see who can stay on the bull the longest! It's behind the Buckaroo Bar!"

Alexis jumped up. "I'll give it a shot!"

"What about Creature?" Jake exclaimed.

"Well, we can't sing to him here," Woodstock said. "People are staring."

Jake looked around. Woodstock was right. He scooped up Creature.

"OK, it might be quieter over there," he said.

As they walked around the Buckaroo Bar, loud excited screams hit Jake. In front of him was a circular arena with a life-size plastic bull in the middle.

Around the edge were rows of shrieking kids. Jake stopped.

"This is a bad idea," he said.

"Oh come on, Jake!" cried Alexis. "Look. There are seats at the back."

Before he could speak, Alexis ran down to the arena. Followed by the others, Jake reluctantly shuffled along the back row and sat down a couple of seats away from a scruffy-looking boy in a cowboy hat. The boy gave him a nod, then looked away.

Jake was about to put the coat-wrapped Creature on the seat next to him, but he paused. *Too risky. That boy might see him.* He tucked Creature carefully under his seat. As he sat back up, a loudspeaker crackled.

"Folks, our final contestant, with a time of fifty-nine seconds to beat . . . let's hear it for . . . Alexis 'Whipcrackin' Williams!"

There were cheers as Alexis ran into the arena. A cowboy handed her a cowboy hat as she climbed onto the bull. The bull started moving, slowly at first, but soon it was bucking madly. Jake held his breath, waiting for Alexis to be thrown off, but she stayed on, gripping the bull with one hand, waving her hat in the air with the other.

Ten seconds . . . twenty . . . thirty . . . Finally, Alexis was thrown off. There was a tense silence, as the cowboy studied his stopwatch.

"Sixty seconds preeeeeecisely! Ladies and Gentlemen, we have a winnerrrrrrrr!"

"GO, ALEXIS!" yelled Nora.

"Shh . . ." Jake hissed, "you'll wake Creature!" He put his hand under his seat and touched a Creature-shaped lump. *He's still asleep.*

The crowd cheered as the cowboy presented Alexis with a piece of paper. She bounded up the arena steps and, talking loudly at top speed, threw herself into the empty seat next to Jake.

"I WON! I WON! I won ice cream for all of us!"

She high-fived Jake, then turned to the boy in the cowboy hat.

"I WON!" she exclaimed. "Isn't that great?"

The boy shrugged.

Alexis looked at him, expectantly, hands on her hips. She clearly felt his response was not good enough.

"Leave him alone, Alexis," Jake whispered. The last thing they wanted was any more attention when they had Creature to deal with.

The boy looked up. "Oh . . . look, I'm sorry. It *is* great. I'm just not having a good day . . ."

Alexis jumped up, still dizzy from her victory.

"What you need is ice cream! And I won free ones! Just wait here." She raced off.

Nora had been listening. She leaned over Jake and spoke to the boy.

"Why aren't you having a good day?" she asked.

"It doesn't matter," he said. "Anyway, I'm glad you guys seem to be enjoying yourselves."

Nora was about to speak again, but her eyes widened and she slowly put her hand over her mouth.

"Oh . . ." she whispered.

Jake slowly looked around.

Hovering vulture-like behind them was Mrs. Blunt.

CHAPTER 9:

HOW TO GET RID OF AN OLD DRAGON

"I spy with my little eye," Mrs. Blunt said in a voice that sent a shiver up Jake's spine, "Six students. But no responsible adult. Where, may I ask, is Mr. Hyde?"

"In the r-restroom, ma'am," Nora peeped.

"Don't lie," Mrs. Blunt snapped. "I have been informed that this group is wandering around without a teacher. Why would Mr. Hyde ignore my —"

PAAAAAAAAAAAARP!

Jake caught a whiff of lime jelly. *Creature had farted . . . again!* He felt Mrs. Blunt's laser eyes burning into the back of his head.

"Aaaaaaaaaaaaaah . . ."

The boy in the cowboy hat let out a long sigh.

Mrs. Blunt's eyes swiveled around instantly. She marched along and rapped on the boy's hat.

"Did you just break wind?" Mrs. Blunt screeched.

The boy stared. "Break what?"

"QUIET! No one breaks wind in front of the principal! It's rule number . . . number . . . whatever number it is, you've earned a Sad Face, young man."

The boy looked confused. "Sad Face?"

Mrs. Blunt pulled a sheet of Sad Face stickers from her bag and slapped one on the boy's cowboy hat. She glared at the hat.

"And *what* is this monstrosity? That's not school dress code."

SLAP. The hat got another sticker.

Jake tried to protest. "Ma'am, he's not —"

"Silence, Jake Jones."

Out of the corner of his eye, Jake spotted Alexis coming back with the ice creams. She stopped abruptly when she saw Mrs. Blunt, who was still ranting.

". . . and Barnaby McCrumb. You've earned yourself a day on the Rockery!"

Barnaby's head shot up. "What have I done?"

"You stole a pair of sunglasses from Amelia Trotter-Hogg."

Barnaby's mouth dropped open. "I found them!"

"He did, ma'am," Karl said.

"Amelia says he stole them," Mrs. Blunt snapped. "And I trust her word."

Jake stood up. Whatever Barnaby had done, he had NOT stolen the sunglasses. What's more, Amelia had clearly forgotten to tell Mrs. Blunt one thing . . .

"Ma'am," Jake said. "Did Amelia tell you that *she* was wandering about alone, without her group, when she lost her sunglasses?"

"Nonsense," Mrs. Blunt said, flustered. "Amelia always sets a good example!"

"Loads of people saw her," Nora added.

A thundercloud was forming just over Mrs. Blunt's head.

"Sheer silliness. Well, Miss Trimble will be able to settle this, won't she! All of you, come with me."

At that moment, Alexis ran forward, ice creams in hand.

"Guess what! I just saw that billionaire guy, Wilfred Wibbly Whatzizname!"

Mrs. Blunt whirled around. The boy in the cowboy hat made an odd snorting noise.

"WHAT? Wilfred Waldo Wellington? Where?" Mrs. Blunt exclaimed.

"In the Buckaroo Bar! He said he was going to the Flower Power Fairy Zone."

"Flower Power . . . are you *sure?*" Mrs. Blunt fluffed up her hair.

"Yes, ma'am. He's giving out free ice cream! Would you like one?" Alexis asked.

"I've got more important things to think about," snapped Mrs. Blunt. "OK, I have to get going. Things to do, billionaires to see."

Mrs. Blunt stalked away.

"That got rid of the old dragon!" Alexis grinned. As she started handing out ice creams, the boy in the cowboy hat spoke.

"Can I —" he began.

"Of course!" Alexis held out an ice cream.

He shook his head, distracted. "Oh, no thanks, I didn't mean —"

"More for me, then!" Barnaby tried to grab the ice cream. Alexis pushed his hand away.

"Get lost, Barnaby —"

"Get lost!" The boy in the cowboy hat repeated. "Who *isn't* lost?" he exclaimed. "The maps are so bad, everywhere I go people are lost, lost, LOST! It's a disaster! No one will . . . wait . . . WHAT IS THAT?"

He pointed to the arena. Jake looked, and his mouth dropped open.

The rodeo bull was starting to move. Perched on its back was Creature!

Everyone gasped. Jake leapt to his feet. *I should never have taken my eyes off him!*

The bull tipped forward.

"JEEPPPERRRRRRRR!"

With a Creaturish battle cry, Creature surfed along the bull's back and swung himself, by its horns, onto the head. The bull flung itself backward.

Creature shot into the air, did three
somersaults, and landed on the bull's bottom.

"Ride 'em cowboy!" Barnaby whooped.

"Ta-dah," Creature squawked smugly, and
bowed. As he did so, the bull lurched again
and Creature did three super-fast forward
rolls along its back, landing back on the head.
A look of enormous surprise crossed his face.

The boy in the cowboy hat roared with laughter.

The bull flung itself from side to side. Creature, clinging to one of the horns, whizzed round and round, faster and faster, till he was a furry blur.

"AH– AH– AH– AH– AAAAAAAARGH!" the furry blur chattered.

The bull lurched forward. With a shriek, Creature was flung high in the air . . .

"YEEEEEEEEE– HA– A– A– A– AAAAAAAA . . . OOMPH!"

He crash-landed in a cloud of dust, tried to stand up, and fell over again, his eyes crossed.

"Now's our chance to grab him," Jake murmured to Nora. But it was too late. Creature scrambled back on the bull.

"No jeeper!" he said firmly. "No jee . . . PER– R– RRRRRRRR!"

The bull bucked violently, throwing Creature even higher. He landed with a clang on the roof of the bull-operating kiosk. This time he didn't try and get back on the bull, just crossed his arms and stared grumpily at it as it slowly came to a halt.

The boy next to Jake wiped his eyes, shaking with laughter.

"That thing should be on TV!" he gasped. "What *is* it?"

Jake thought quickly. "He's, um, just one of the Alien Zone workers."

The boy stopped laughing. His eyes narrowed.

"You're not telling me the truth. What's your name?" he demanded.

"Jake," Jake said uneasily.

The boy turned to Nora. "And you?"

"I'm Nora," she said. "This is Alexis, Karl, and Barnaby."

The boy nodded. His face very thoughtful. *Why has he gone all grown up and formal?* Jake wondered. *Who is this kid?*

"And you are . . . ?" Jake asked.

The boy smiled.

"My name is Wilf."

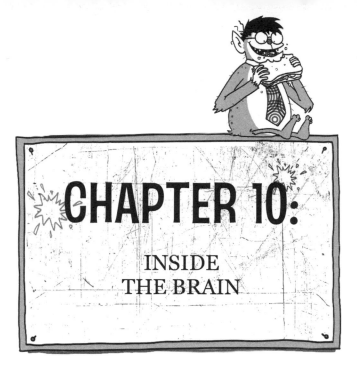

CHAPTER 10:

INSIDE
THE BRAIN

Nora, Karl, Alexis, and Woodstock gasped.
Jake's jaw dropped.

"*The* Wilf?" he stammered.

"Just Wilf is fine," Wilf said, grinning.

The scruffy boy was none other than
Wilfred Waldo Wellington, Jr., eccentric
billionaire and owner of the adventure park!

Alexis looked doubtful. "You don't *look*
like a billionaire!"

"I'm in disguise," Wilf said. "I wanted to walk around without anyone recognizing me."

"Why?" Barnaby asked. "Would they ask for money?"

Wilf laughed. "No, I wanted to see what people really thought of the park. I wandered around all morning and all I heard was, 'We're lost! These maps are useless!' So I came here to think what to do. But then all of you turned up and your loopy principal arrived and that crazy creature appeared . . . speaking of which . . ."

Creature! Jake had almost forgotten about him! His eyes darted to the kiosk. Creature was still on the kiosk roof, sulking.

We have to catch him, he thought. *But that would mean telling Wilf.*

"It is yours, isn't it?" Wilf said, watching Jake closely. "I know it's not a worker from the Alien Zone!"

There was a sudden wild cackle.

"Creature!" cried Nora. Jake turned to see Creature bounding out of the arena!

He jumped up. The others jumped up too.

"Sorry, Wilf! No time to explain!"

They raced back to the entrance of the arena, but Creature was already bouncing off into the distance. Jake started after him, but Wilf grabbed his arm.

"You'll never catch up," Wilf said. "Look, I can help you, but you have to tell me everything."

Jake gulped. "OK . . ."

"You must swear not to tell anyone, though," Nora said.

"I swear," Wilf said.

"Well," Jake said, slowly, "Mr. Hyde, our teacher, he sort of, well . . . he turns . . ."

Jake paused. "Into a . . ."

"Creature!" finished Barnaby.

Wilf stared. "That creature is your teacher?"

They all nodded. Jake looked at Wilf. *Will he be angry? Disbelieving? Laugh and think it a joke?*

But Wilf grabbed Jake's arm, an excited gleam in his eye.

"Really?" he asked, breathlessly. "How? Can anyone do it? Could *I* do it?"

Jake was taken aback. "Err . . . I don't think so."

Wilf looked disappointed. "Oh well. I'd like to have been able to change into a creature! So will he change back into a teacher?"

"Yes," said Jake. "But we've got to help him to do it before the opening ceremony at one o'clock! That's when the principal will see he's not there and we won't be able to cover that up . . . he'll lose his job."

Wilf looked at his watch. "It's half past eleven now. OK, I've got an idea. Follow me."

He ran to an electric golf cart that was parked at the back of the Buckaroo Bar.

"Jump in!" he called.

They all squished in. Wilf stepped on a pedal and the cart hummed smoothly off.

Groups of people stepped out of their way and stared curiously at them as they drove past.

"Creature didn't go this way!" Alexis said.

"Trust me!" said Wilf, scooting around a corner. The cart came to a stop. "Here we are."

Jake looked up. A huge pink thing loomed before them. It looked like . . .

"A BRAIN!" exclaimed Nora. "That's what that pink blob on the map was!"

Wilf flushed. "I'm hopeless at drawing."

"How did you design the park then?" asked Woodstock.

"You'll see in a minute," said Wilf, jumping down from the cart. "This is the Brain, my control center. Come on!"

Following Wilf into the Brain, they found themselves in a huge, brightly lit room. One wall was a collection of screens. In the middle of the room was a round pit filled with toy building bricks, and to one side of this stood a complicated building brick structure. Jake walked over and saw it was a perfect model of the whole park.

"Awesome!" said Woodstock. He got out his sketchbook and started doodling.

"That's how I designed the park," said Wilf. "But there's no time . . . GENIE!"

A silver robot came gliding toward them.

"Hi, Wilf," said the robot. "What is your wish?"

"Cameras, please," said Wilf. Immediately, the wall of screens flickered into life.

"There are cameras all over the park," explained Wilf. "If we look long enough, we should be able to find your creature . . . teacher."

They spread out along the wall and stared at the screens. On one screen, Jake spotted Mrs. Blunt chasing a smartly dressed man carrying ice creams. But no Creature.

"Here!" yelled Karl.

Everyone rushed over.

All Jake could see on the screen was a wailing child holding an empty hot dog bun.

"Where?" asked Jake.

Creature's face suddenly appeared on the next screen. He was covered in ketchup and a hot dog was hanging out of his mouth. He slurped it in, burped at the camera, and disappeared again.

Jake shook his head. "We've lost him."

"No we haven't!" cried Alexis, pointing at another screen.

A bald man was clutching his head and waving his fist. Two seconds later, on the next screen, Creature appeared, now wearing a wig.

Barnaby started laughing. Nora groaned. "He's being naughtier than ever!"

Wilf spoke to the robot.

"Two walkie-talkies, please, Genie!"

"Your wish is my command," said the robot, gliding off.

Wilf turned to Jake.

"You take a walkie-talkie and go after Creature. I'll take one and watch the screens. Then I can tell you right where he is."

"Great idea!" said Alexis.

"We'll need maps, though," said Jake.

Wilf hit himself on the head. "But you can't use the maps! You'll get lost . . ."

"No we won't!"

Everyone looked around. Woodstock was holding up his sketchbook.

Wilf blinked. "What's that?"

"A map of the park," said Woodstock, handing it to Wilf. "Only with everything in the right place."

"But how . . ." Wilf looked astonished.

"Easy! I just copied the toy model," said Woodstock.

"Easy? I wouldn't be able to . . . anyway, it's awesome!"

Woodstock flushed with pride.

Wilf handed Woodstock's map to the robot, who had just returned with the walkie-talkies.

"Quick, Genie. I need six copies of this please. We've got a Creature to catch!"

CHAPTER 11:

MONKEY MAYHEM

Jake and his friends sprinted out of the Brain control center.

"It's 12:30," said Nora. "We've got half an hour."

Wilf's voice came over Jake's walkie-talkie.

"Jake, can you hear me?"

Jake pushed the *Talk* button. "Yes . . ."

"Creature's in the Wildlife Zone, heading for Monkey Mayhem. Can you see it on the map?"

Nora peered at her map. "Got it!"

Following the map, they soon came to
a building with a roof shaped like a banana.
A sign read:

MONKEY MAYHEM

"There's another entrance at the back,"
Woodstock said, pointing at the map.

"We'll have more chance of catching
him if we split up," Alexis said.

"OK," Jake said. "Three of us will go in this way . . ."

"I'll come with you," Nora said.

Woodstock stepped forward. "Me too."

Karl looked at Alexis and Barnaby. "We'll go around the back then."

As Karl, Alexis, and Barnaby disappeared, Nora pushed the door open. Jake groaned.

"It's just like a jungle!"

It was as if they had walked into a tropical rain forest. Huge trees towered on every side, and from their branches swung a chattering, messy mob of monkeys.

"He could be anywhere!" said Nora. "This is not good."

"Worse. Look who's turned up," said Woodstock.

Heading toward them from the other end of the monkey house was Amelia's group. It was too late to run or hide. Amelia had spotted them.

"HEY! Jake Jones!"

Amelia charged toward Jake like a rampaging rhino.

"WHY DID YOU TELL ON ME TO MRS. BLUNT?" she shrieked.

Several monkeys fell out of their trees in fright. Jake opened his mouth to speak, but at that moment Miss Trimble hurried up with the rest of the group.

"Now, children, I'm sure this can be resolved by non-violent means —"

SPLAT!!!

A large rotten mango fell out of a tree and exploded on Amelia's head.

"Aaaaaargh!" she screamed.

SQUELCH! SQUISH! SPLAT!

Jake jumped back as several more mangoes splatted down on Amelia's group. One landed on the unfortunate Miss Trimble's head and was followed by several very overripe bananas. Miss Trimble stood rooted to the spot as past-its-sell-by-date fruit salad slid down her ears.

She sank to the floor.

"Ohhhh" the teacher moaned. "I think I'm having one of my funny moods . . ."

Amelia stood quivering with fury, mango juice dribbling down her face. Jake, Nora, and Woodstock dodged through the rain of fruit to help Miss Trimble.

"Is it the end of the world, children?" she asked in a shaky voice.

"No, Miss, it's a monkey throwing mangoes," said Jake, hauling her to her feet. A few feet away, a huge palm leaf jutted out over the path.

"Under there!" he said.

They bundled
Miss Trimble
under the shelter
of the palm leaf.
Jake peered out.
Through the
leaves, he could just see the monkey who was
throwing fruit.

It was a very large, greenish monkey, and it
was wearing glasses and a wig. Thanks to the
green gloop he was well camouflaged by the
leaves.

"That's no monkey up there, that's
Creature!" Jake called out to Woodstock and
Nora.

Several real monkeys were perched a few
branches away, gazing at Creature in awe.

Amelia gave a yelp and ducked as another banana whizzed past her ear.

She picked up the banana and threw it back to where Creature and the monkeys were sitting. Immediately, Creature's fan club of monkeys launched a shower of bananas in her direction.

"HELP!" she screamed, fending off the hail of fruit.

Jake grabbed her too and pulled her under the leaf. Then he spotted Karl and Alexis coming through the back door and running toward them.

"What's going on?" exclaimed Alexis, looking around in astonishment.

"Monkeys throwing fruit. Where's Barnaby?" asked Jake.

Karl looked around. "He came in through a side door. He should be here."

Amelia crossed her arms. "So now there's no Barnaby and there's no Mr. Hyde? Just wait till I tell Mrs. Blunt!"

She barged out from under the leaf. "Come on, my group!"

Amelia's group filed after her. But Miss Trimble didn't move. She was still sitting under the palm leaf, talking to a banana. Amelia came marching back.

"Come on, Miss Trimble!" she snapped. "We've got to find Mrs. Blunt!"

Miss Trimble peered up at her. "Blunt? Well sharpen it, dear!"

Amelia stared. "I said 'Mrs. Blunt!' Have you got mango in your ear?"

Miss Trimble choked. "What? My rear is just fine, thank you."

"YOUR EAR!" shouted Amelia. "Oh, let's just go."

She marched back toward the door.

Woodstock and Nora helped Miss Trimble up. She smiled vaguely at them and held up her banana.

"This is Boris," she said. "He's going to help me make banana cream pie!"

Jake and the others watched, as she tottered off after Amelia, leaving a trail of mango juice behind her.

"She's gone a bit loopy — fruit loopy!" said Karl.

Alexis giggled.

"Don't be mean. Should we go with her?" asked Nora. Two Class 5A students were helping Miss Trimble out of the door.

"Her group will look after her," said Jake. "We've got to catch Creature."

Karl looked at his watch. "And we only have fifteen minutes to do it!"

"Come on, then!" Jake turned toward the tree where Creature had been.

Creature and his fan club had vanished. But Barnaby was leaning against the trunk, a mischievous grin on his face.

"Barnaby!" exclaimed Nora. "Where in the world *were* you?"

Barnaby shrugged. "I didn't want to get mangoed, so I hid behind a tree."

Jake was furious. "You could have helped us out!"

Barnaby blinked.

"Jake stood up for you to Mrs. Blunt earlier," Woodstock said.

Barnaby's grin faded. Jake thought he looked a bit guilty.

"Oh, yeah. Sorry."

Alexis glared at him. "We have to work together, or we'll never catch Creature."

Just then, Wilf's voice crackled over Jake's walkie-talkie.

"Jake! You've got to get to the Crocodile Pool! Creature's trying to feed bananas to the crocodile!"

CHAPTER 12:

DO NOT FEED THE CROCODILE!

"Come on!" Alexis sped off, Jake and the others hot on her heels. They burst out of the monkey house.

"Which way, Nora?" Woodstock shouted.

She scanned the map. "Straight on!"

In a couple of minutes they reached a high wire fence with a large sign on it.

Creature was perched on the fence, flinging bananas into the crocodile pool.

DO NOT FEED THE CROCODILE!

"Wheeeeee . . ." PLOP! "Wheeeeee . . ."

Creature squawked when he saw the six students approaching and hopped down into the enclosure.

"GET OUT, CREATURE!" yelled Jake, slamming against the fence.

"Do you want to be lunch?" shouted Alexis. "There's a crocodile in there!"

Creature cackled, stuck two bananas in his ears, and bounded to the pool. A huge knotted log was floating in it. Creature hurled himself onto one end of the log, causing it to rock dangerously.

Creature laughed, and bounced up and down.

"BOING! BOING! BOING!"

Then he stood on one leg and pretended to be a ballet dancer.

"Tra-la-laaaa . . . ahhhhhh . . ."
Creature's eyes widened. He looked down.

". . . aaaaaaaaaaaaaHHHHH!"

The end of the log where Creature was pirouetting was rising into the air!

"ARR-AAAAR-R-R-R?!?" croaked the log.

"THE LOG!" shouted Karl. "IT'S A CROCODILE!"

Everyone screamed. Jake's legs turned to jelly. Creature was pirouetting on the huge scaly nose of the biggest crocodile Jake had ever seen!

The crocodile's yellow eyes fixed on Creature.

Creature chattered noisily. He pulled the bananas out of his ears . . .

Nora shouted, "Whatever you do . . ."

. . . and stuck them in the crocodile's cave-like nostrils.

". . . don't make it angry!"

"AR- AR- ARRAAAARR- RR- R!"

The crocodile made a noise like a T. Rex that had swallowed a power drill. It jerked its head back, tossing Creature and the bananas into the air. Then, with a powerful flick of its tail, it whacked Creature right across the enclosure. The six friends watched, horrified, as he slammed against the fence on the other side and slid to the ground in a daze.

The crocodile glided through the water toward Creature.

He'll be eaten alive! There was only one thing to do.

Jake scrambled up the fence.

"What are you doing?" shouted Karl.

"I'm going in," Jake shouted, jumping over. "I'll distract it, get it to come this way."

Nora scrambled over too.

"I'm coming," she said. "I'll try to talk to it"

"Nora, you can't *talk* to a croc!"

"*I* can. Come on . . ."

They ran to the pool. The crocodile was crawling up the bank toward Creature.

"OVER HERE!" shouted Jake.

The crocodile kept crawling.

Jake swallowed. *I'll have to get closer.* The pool looked shallow enough. He stepped in, and sank up to his waist in cold, muddy water.

"Aaarrrrahhhh-ah-ah-ahhhh!"
croaked Nora.

The crocodile looked around.

"What did you say?" hissed Jake.

"'We are your friends,' I think . . . I've only ever tested it on frogs though."

With a sharp turn, the crocodile slid back into the water and began to glide straight toward Jake!

"I don't *want* to be its friend!" panted Jake, trying to clamber out. But his foot had got tangled up in seaweed! His ears started pounding painfully.

"I'm stuck!"

"Grab my hand!" Nora cried. Jake grabbed it. Nora pulled. Jake felt his foot break free.

"Aaaaaaaaaaaaaaargh!" Nora's feet shot out from under her! With a scream, she plunged into the pool and disappeared under the water.

Jake heaved her up, floundering and gasping. A few feet away, he could see the crocodile getting closer . . . and closer . . .

"JEEPPPPPPPERRRRRRRRRR!"

A brown fur ball landed WHUMP! on the tip of the crocodile's nose. Nora gasped.

"Creature!"

"AAARRRRRR?!" the crocodile grunted in shock. He swung his head from side to side in a frenzy, trying to shake Creature off. But Creature had learned a few tricks from the rodeo bull! He hung on, hollering like a cowboy.

"Yeeee-hawwwwwww!"

The crocodile got angrier and angrier, lashing the water up into a muddy froth.

We have to get out! With a massive effort, Jake tried to heave Nora up the bank, but she kept on slipping back down.

SNAP!

The crocodile's mouth snapped shut. Jake and Nora whirled around.

Creature was nowhere to be seen.

"You bully! You ate him!" screamed Nora.

The crocodile began to open its mouth again. But at that moment a small, bedraggled, bespectacled cannonball burst out of the water and threw itself toward Jake and Nora.

"**Jeeppppeerrrrrrrrrr!**" Creature growled at the crocodile.

Jake gaped. *He's protecting us!* This scraggy little bundle of mischief was standing up to a monster crocodile — for him and Nora!

What was it that Mr. Hyde had said about friends . . . ?

The crocodile's eyes gleamed. Then it surged toward Creature.

"FRIENDS STICK TOGETHER!" Jake shouted. He and Nora charged at the crocodile and grabbed Creature. Jake raised a fist. "Get out of here, you overgrown lizard!" he cried.

The crocodile didn't seem to like being called an overgrown lizard. It started to open its mouth and lunged forward. Jake closed his eyes . . .

"CROCCY! COOKIES!"

Jake's eyes snapped open. He saw Barnaby and Karl on one side of the pool, hurling cookies at the crocodile.

The crocodile stopped moving, confused.

Then there was a shout. "HEY!"

Jake whirled around. Alexis and Woodstock were on the other side of the pool, beating sticks together and yelling at the top of their lungs.

The crocodile swung its head from side to side. It was not sure where to look.

"Keep going, everyone!" shouted Jake. "I think it's working! We're really confusing him."

They carried on. As the crocodile became more and more disorientated, Jake felt warmth coming off the soggy Creature.

Nora gasped. "He's glowing!"

It was true. Creature was bathed in orange light. Soon, every hair on his body was glowing. Sparks flew off him.

"OW!" Jake and Nora let go of the now red-hot Creature, who rolled back into the water.

CRACK!!

A bolt of lightning shot out from his tail and struck the crocodile on the nose.

"AAA-AAAA-AAAARGGGH!"

roared the crocodile. Its nose smoking, the huge reptile turned and slipped under the surface of the pool.

The water frothed and churned . . . the smell of burning rubber filled the air . . .

FAAAAAAAAAAAAARRRRRT!

Wheeeeeeee · · · · · · · · · · · ·

POP! POP! POP!

BANG!

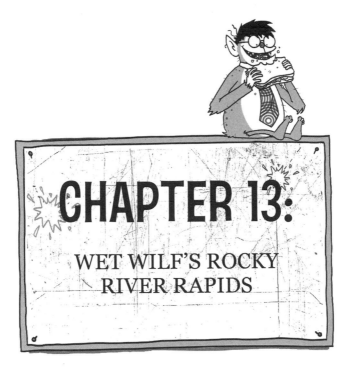

CHAPTER 13:

WET WILF'S ROCKY RIVER RAPIDS

"Jake, Nora! Grab these!"

Karl, Barnaby, Woodstock, and Alexis were at the top of the bank, pushing branches down to the water. Jake and Nora grabbed them and were dragged, shaken and dripping, up the slope.

"Creature's changed!" Jake managed to gasp as he collapsed onto the bank.

"Yeah," said Barnaby, grinning. "It was quite a show!"

Karl pointed. Jake turned.

Standing knee deep in steaming mud was Mr. Hyde, muddy but back to normal. He took off his muddy glasses, wiped them on his muddy jacket, and put them back on, still muddy. He peered up at the students on the bank staring at him. Then he looked down at himself.

"Oh no," he groaned. "I didn't do anything too . . . silly, did I?"

Jake paused. "Well . . ."

He was saved from answering by a shout.

"CONAN! Where's Conan?"

Jake turned, to see Wilf running toward them.

"Who's Conan?" asked Woodstock.

Wilf screeched to a halt beside them.

"The crocodile," he panted. "Conan is completely harmless. He's got no teeth!"

Everyone stared.

"No teeth?" said Nora, amazed. "How did we not notice that?"

Jake laughed. "You normally notice everything!"

Nora looked annoyed. "I was a teensy bit terrified, remember?"

Wilf looked mortified. "I tried to tell you over the walkie-talkie, but it went dead! It must have got water in it!" He looked around. "Where is he?"

Alexis pointed. "Over there."

The terrified, toothless crocodile had left the water and was hiding behind a tree on the far bank.

Wilf turned to Jake. "Sorry, I should have told you earlier. We're having a set of false teeth made for him, but at the moment all he can eat is soup!"

"Ahem. Could someone give me a hand, please?"

A soggy Mr. Hyde was trying to climb out of the pool. Together, they pulled him up the bank.

"So you're the one who can turn into a creature!" said Wilf, gazing wonderingly at the teacher. Mr. Hyde gave Jake a worried look.

"Sir, this is Wilf, the park owner," said Jake, pointing to his new friend.

"He swore not to tell on you," said Nora, giving Wilf a stern look.

"I won't," said Wilf. His walkie-talkie suddenly crackled. He picked it up. "Genie?"

A robotic voice spoke:

"Opening ceremony in five minutes."

Jake slapped his head. *The opening ceremony!* He'd almost forgotten it, in all the chaos.

"We've got to go!" he cried. "I'd rather face a croc than Mrs. Blunt if we're not there at one o'clock!"

"We won't make it," groaned Karl. "We're miles from the entrance!"

Wilf looked thoughtful.

"There might be a way . . ."

He ran to the fence and climbed over. Mystified, Jake and his friends followed. Wilf pointed to a gate just across from the crocodile enclosure.

A sign over the gate read:

WET WILF'S
ROCKY RIVER RAPIDS

"The fastest ride in the park," said Wilf, proudly. "It goes around the edge of the Wildlife Zone and finishes at the entrance!"

"Genius!" exclaimed Woodstock.

They ran through the gate and up a steep flight of steps, emerging next to a narrow channel of water, with canoes bobbing in a line. At the end was a sudden drop, from which came the sound of rushing water.

Wilf began unhooking canoes.

"Nora and Alexis, you first," he said. They jumped in the first canoe and Wilf gave it a mighty shove.

Barnaby and Karl got in the next one. Jake helped push them, whooping, over the edge.

"Jake and Mr. Hyde, you next!"

Jake helped his teacher into the canoe and jumped into the front seat. Wilf and Woodstock pushed the canoe out.

Even under his layer of mud, Mr. Hyde looked pale.

"Hold tight, sir," shouted Jake. "WHOA . . ."

For one heart-stopping moment, the canoe teetered on the brink . . .

SPLOOSH!!

The canoe slammed into the water and plunged down what seemed like an almost vertical drop!

"OOOOOOHHHHHH!" yelled Mr. Hyde.
The bottom was coming up toward them,
fast. Too fast! Jake crouched lower in his seat
and covered his head, holding his breath . . .

WHUMP! A wall of water hit the canoe.
Jake felt it wash over him.

"Gleuuuurgghhhh!" gurgled Mr. Hyde,
who hadn't ducked. The front of the canoe
was underwater. *They were going to capsize!*
But by some miracle, the canoe righted itself.
Jake barely had time to take a breath when
the canoe veered sharply to one side. *Ouch!*

His neck twisted. The canoe swung back the other way. The banks were getting higher and higher. They were being sucked into a dark, narrow gorge. Sharp rocks reared up out of the water ahead.

"Are we almost there?" he heard Mr. Hyde yell, his voice echoing off the steep walls.

"I don't know!" Jake yelled back.

The canoe rocketed along, faster and faster, dodging the rocks with inches to spare. The gorge got narrower and narrower. Then Jake gasped — straight ahead was a huge rock!

They were going to crash right into it!

Jake closed his eyes. *Five . . . four . . . three . . . two . . . one . . .*

But the crash never came. Jake opened his eyes just in time to see the rock split open, straight down the middle! The canoe shot through and Jake found they were floating gently along a calm, narrow channel.

Amazingly, the canoe slowly came to rest beside a wooden platform.

Nora, Alexis, Karl, and Barnaby ran to help him and Mr. Hyde out.

"Mr. Hyde, you're nice and clean again!" exclaimed Nora.

It was true. Mr. Hyde was dripping wet like the rest of them, but there was no longer a trace of mud or green gloop on him.

"Hurry," called Alexis. "Two minutes left!"

"Hang on. Look! Here come Wilf and
Woodstock," said Jake.

The rock opened again, and the last canoe
shot through and floated up to the platform.

There was no one in it!

CHAPTER 14:

THE GRAND OPENING CEREMONY

They stared at the empty canoe.

"They must have fallen out!" gasped Nora.

Jake peered upriver, but the rock had closed, blocking his view.

Mr. Hyde clutched his head and groaned. "This is a disaster! We'll have to go back."

"Wait, what's this?" Jake fished a piece of paper from the bottom of the empty canoe.

It looked like a page from Woodstock's sketchbook.

Everyone crowded around as he opened it.

"It just says 'Go!'" said Jake.

"So let's go, then!" said Barnaby.

Jake tugged a reluctant Mr. Hyde through the gate. Ahead, he saw the Spaceport building where they had first come in. A crowd of excited people swarmed around a podium which had been placed to one side of it. At the front, Jake spotted Mrs. Blunt, glaring as she scanned the area.

Looking for Mr. Hyde, Jake thought. He grabbed his teacher's arm, and they pushed through the crowd. As they neared Mrs. Blunt, Jake heard a shrill voice.

"THERE THEY ARE, MA'AM! I bet you anything that Mr. Hyde's not . . ."

Amelia's voice faltered.

"Hello, Amelia," said Mr. Hyde, cheerily.

"MR. HYDE!" exploded Mrs. Blunt. "Why haven't you been with your group all day?"

"He has, ma'am," said Jake. "He just had to, um, go to the bathroom . . ."

". . . a lot," finished Barnaby.

Mr. Hyde caught on. "Yes, must have been something I ate." There was a loud rumble. He looked pained. "Oh dear! That only happens when I have awful gas . . ."

Mrs. Blunt turned pale and backed away. "Please! I've heard enough." Mrs. Blunt pivoted on her very-high-heeled shoes, and scurried away with urgency.

"Ma'am, ma'am . . ." Amelia was jumping up and down, trying to get Mrs. Blunt's attention. "There's a student missing . . ."

At that moment, the crowd gave an excited gasp. "Oooooooooooh!"

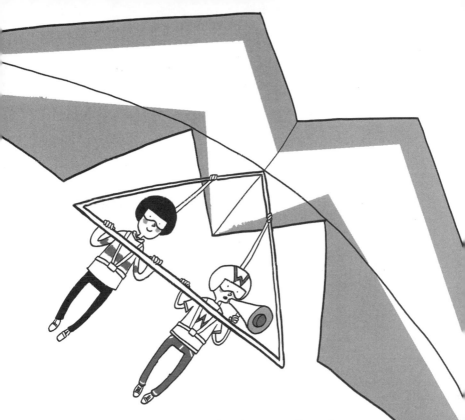

Everyone was pointing at the sky.

Jake looked up and saw a huge W-shaped hang-glider floating toward them. Suspended beneath it were two figures in helmets and goggles.

As it came closer, Jake gasped. *Was it . . . ?*

"W for Wilf!" shouted Barnaby.

"And W for Woodstock!" laughed Nora.

The W swooped lower. Even though the two figures were helmeted, Jake could see that they were, indeed, Wilf and Woodstock! Wilf called through a megaphone.

"GREETINGS, EVERYONE! WELCOME TO MY ADVENTURE PARK!"

The hang-glider circled lower and lower till it landed with a gentle bump in front of the podium. There was a ripple of applause.

Wilf and Woodstock started to unstrap themselves.

"MISTER WELLINGTON!"

Mrs. Blunt was barging her way through the crowd.

"It *is* Mr. Wellington, isn't it?" she said, stopping in front of Wilf and looking him up and down.

He nodded, slightly reluctantly Jake thought. "Yes . . . that's me."

"I thought you'd be taller . . . anyway, I *do* hope you remember me," she went on. "My name is Mrs. Blunt. I wrote asking if you could donate some money toward an exciting project for my humble little school? Some of the students have already raised quite a lot. Young Woodstock, for example . . . Where is that boy?"

Woodstock took off his helmet and goggles. Mrs. Blunt looked surprised.

"Well, I see you two have met! Woodstock, go ahead and tell Mr. Wellington about our worthy cause."

Woodstock looked Mrs. Blunt straight in the eye.

"Mrs. Blunt, I've explained everything to Wilf. *I* collected money for a new art studio. But *you* want to put it toward a bunch of boring statues of principals!"

"Oh dear . . ." murmured the crowd.

Mrs. Blunt began to flush red.

Wilf pulled his goggles up, and looked at Mrs. Blunt.

"I *do* remember you," he said. "You're the lady who accused me of farting."

"Oh dear . . ." gasped the crowd, louder.

Mrs. Blunt's eyes bulged.

"YOU?" she gasped. "That — that scruffy boy at Rockin' Roger's Rodeo? *You* are Wilfred Waldo Wellington, Jr.?"

"Just Wilf is fine," said Wilf. "Now, if you'll excuse me . . ." He climbed onto the podium and spoke into a microphone.

"Welcome to the Grand Opening of Wacky Wilf's Wild Adventure Park! I know there have been problems with the maps today, and I want to make that right. May I introduce my new map-making assistant — WOODSTOCK STONE!"

"HURRAY!" yelled the crowd.

Woodstock looked almost as shocked as Mrs. Blunt.

"M-me?" he gasped.

Wilf hadn't finished. "It's a paid job. I'll triple the money you've raised for the art studio . . ."

Woodstock's eyes nearly popped out.

". . . but the money has to go toward an art studio, not statues."

"HURRAY AGAIN!" The crowd went wild.

Mrs. Blunt didn't go wild. She went a ghastly shade of white.

"And if it's OK with you, I'd love to design the art studio myself, with some help from my friends," said Wilf, grinning cheekily at Jake and the others.

He turned, then turned back. "Nearly forgot. I declare this park to be . . . OPEN!"

Wilf ran to join Jake and the others. Mr. Hyde clapped him on the back. "Marvelous gesture, young Wilf."

A band suddenly started playing loud, funky music. Mr. Hyde's eyes lit up.

"Wonderful! I love a boogie!" Mr. Hyde started twitching is body to the beat.

"Who wants to dance?" cried Mr. Hyde. He spotted Miss Trimble. She was wandering around in a daze, telling everyone her secret recipe for banana cream pie.

"Three eggs . . ."

"Miss Trimble! Care for a dance?"

She peered at him.

"A spoonful of sugar . . ." Mr. Hyde grabbed Miss Trimble. "Helps the medicine go down!" sang Mr. Hyde. He whirled her round so her feet flew up in the air.

"Then . . . add . . . bananas . . ." gasped Miss Trimble, whizzing around faster and faster with Mr. Hyde.

"Look!" Nora nudged Jake. He turned to see Mrs. Blunt being helped to a bench by park staff. Amelia was running alongside her.

"MA'AM! You've got to do something, ma'am! Why don't you . . . ?"

Jake grinned at Nora. She was about to say something, when . . .

Fizzzzzzzzzz . . . POP!!

The crowd ooohed. "Fireworks!"

"Fireworks? In the daytime?" Nora said, puzzled.

POP! POP! POP!

Jake sniffed. *Those fireworks smell odd, kind of like . . . burning rubber?* He spun around.

"That's not fireworks! That's . . ."

"BANANA CREAM PIEEEEEEEE!" shrieked Miss Trimble, flying through the air. Mr. Hyde's coat lay in a steaming pile on the ground.

Jake and Nora looked at each other in horror.

"Oh no! Not again, Mr. Hyde!"

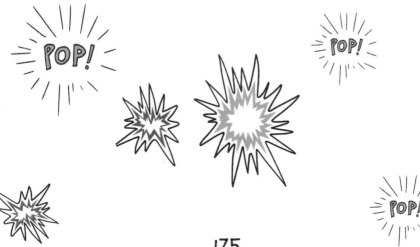

ABOUT THE AUTHOR

Sam Watkins voraciously consumed books from a young age, due to a food shortage in the village where she grew up. This diet, although not recommended by doctors, has given her a lifelong passion for books. She has been a bookseller, editor, and publisher, and writes and illustrates her own children's books. At one point, things all got a bit too bookish so she decided to be an art teacher for a while, but books won the day in the end.

ABOUT THE ILLUSTRATOR

David O'Connell is an illustrator who lives in London, England. His favorite things to draw are monsters, naughty children (another type of monster), batty old ladies, and evil cats . . . Oh, and teachers that transform into naughty little creatures!